THE NEW KID

For Anton

Copyright © 1989 American Teacher Publications
Published by Raintree Publishers Limited Partnership

Library of Congress number: 89-3689

Library of Congress Cataloging in Publication Data

Economos, Chris.
  The new kid / Chris Economos; illustrated by Steve McInturff.

  (Real readers)
  Summary: A chimpanzee substitutes for a sick baseball player.
  [1. Baseball—Fiction. 2. Chimpanzees—Fiction.] I. McInturff, Steve, ill. II. Title.
III. Series.
PZ7.E2125Ne 1989   [E]—dc19   89-3689
ISBN: 0-8172-3512-4

   2 3 4 5 6 7 8 9 0   93 92 91 90

REAL READERS

THE NEW KID

by Chris Economos
illustrated by Steve McInturff

Raintree Publishers
Milwaukee

It was a good day to play baseball, but Jane was not happy. How could she tell her friends that the game was off?

"Jane," Tom said, "what's up? Why are you so sad?"

"Dan just called me," said Jane. "He can't play today."

"But we can't play without Dan," said Tom. "We need another kid. What will we do?"

Just then they saw a girl playing ball with a woman.

"I know that woman," said Jane. "She just moved in on my street. And that must be her kid she's playing ball with. Let's ask the new kid if she wants to play on our team."

But when they went to ask her, they saw that the new kid was not a kid at all.

"The new kid is a monkey!" said Tom.

"This is Cindy," said the woman. "She is my pet chimp. She's very good at catching balls. And she can hit them, too."

"She's just what we need!" said Jane. "Can she play ball on our team today?"

The woman said, "Yes. I think Cindy would like that."

Jane, Tom, and Cindy tossed the ball as they waited for the rest of the kids to show up. Cindy was very good at catching the ball.

One after another, the other kids showed up. Rick was the last kid to get there. They all had to wait for him. He had the bat.

Rick and his team laughed when they saw Cindy. "Who is that?" Rick asked.

"You mean what is that!" laughed Dawn.

"This is Cindy," said Jane. "Dan can't play today, so Cindy is going to take his place. She's the new kid on our team."

"Let Cindy play," laughed Rick. "How can you win with a monkey playing on your team?"

Rick's team was up first, and Rick was the first kid up at bat. He picked up his bat. Then he went to home plate.

"I am going to hit that ball all the way down the block!" Rick said.

Rick waited for the ball to come. He swung at it. He hit it! The ball went up and up.

Rick ran for first base.

But Cindy ran and jumped up. She got the ball.

"Rick is out!" yelled Tom. "Good girl, Cindy! That's the way to play!"

Two more times, kids from Rick's team hit the ball. And two more times Cindy jumped up and got the ball.

Then it was time for Jane's team to be up at bat.

Jane went up to home plate. She waited for the ball. She swung at it. She hit it! Jane ran to first base.

"Look at Jane," said the woman to Cindy "Can you do what she did?"

Cindy nodded. She jumped up and down.

Then Tom went up to bat. He swung at the ball. He hit it! He ran to first base.

"Look at Tom," said the woman to Cindy.

"Can you do what he did?"

Cindy nodded. She jumped up and down.

Then it was Cindy's turn to be up at bat.

"Go on, Cindy," said the woman. "Do what the other kids did. You can do it! Go hit the ball."

Cindy nodded. She jumped up and got the bat. She went to home plate and waited for the ball.

Rick laughed. "Maybe Cindy can catch a ball, but I bet she can't hit one," he said.

The ball came, Cindy swung at it. She hit it! The ball went up and up and UP!

Jane ran to home plate. She made it! Then Tom ran to home plate. And then, last of all, Cindy!

"We have 3 runs now!" said Jane. "Good girl, Cindy! That's the way to play!"

"What will we do now?" Dawn asked Rick. "Jane's team is going to win!"

Rick was mad. "Look," he said. "This isn't fair. Cindy can't play!"

"Why not?" asked Jane.

"Cindy is a monkey," said Rick. "It isn't fair for a monkey to play."

"It is fair!" said Jane. "I will tell you why. I am little. You are little. Cindy is little, too. So it's fair that Cindy plays."

"OK, OK," said Rick. "Cindy can play. But why does Cindy get to play on your team? We want her to play for us."

Just then the woman got up. "You kids need help!" she said. "And I know just what you need. Wait here, I'll be back soon."

When the woman came back, she had a little chimp with her. This new chimp looked just like Cindy!

"This is Sammy," said the woman. "He likes to play ball, too."

"Come on, Sammy," said Rick. "Let's play ball! You can be the new kid on our team."

Sharing the Joy of Reading

Beginning readers enjoy reading books on their own. Reading a book is a worthwhile activity in and of itself for a young reader. However, a child's reading can be even more rewarding if it is shared. This sharing can enhance your child's appreciation—both of the book and of his or her own abilities.

  Now that your child has read **The New Kid**, you can help extend your child's reading experience by encouraging him or her to:

- Retell the story or key concepts presented in this story in his or her own words. The retelling can be oral or written.

- Create a picture of a favorite character, event, or concept from this book.

- Express his or her own ideas and feelings about the characters in this book and other things the characters might do.

Here is a special activity that you and your child can do together to further extend the appreciation of this book: Cindy the chimp was able to hit a home run because she imitated what the children were doing. You and your child can play an imitation game together. Sit or stand facing your child. Say "One, two, three—make a funny face!" and make a funny face for your child to imitate. Then encourage your child to make his or her own funny face on the count of three, while you try to imitate it. This game can be played by making funny faces, funny gestures, or by saying or singing words. The importance is in the *imitation* of the action or words.